DRAGON JELLY

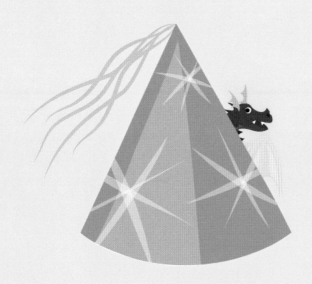

Claire Freedman   Illustrated by **Sue Hendra**
and **Paul Linnet**

BLOOMSBURY

LONDON   NEW DELHI   NEW YORK   SYDNEY

Come to Max's MONSTER party.
There's GOO-LICIOUS food to eat!

It's creepy-crawly, stinky fun —
don't miss the SCARY treat!

First it's monster pass-the-parcel,
which squiggles, shakes and squirms,

and when the final wrapper's off,
they find a nest of worms!

The hairy green magician
makes frogspawn disappear.

Kapow! As if by magic,
frogs hop from Max's ear!

Hooray! It's bouncy castle time,
but this one's extra mucky.

As the monsters jump and bump,
it sprays out gunk — SPLAT-YUCKY!

The monsters need to cool right down.
Quick! To the paddling pool.

It slops with buzzing botfly eggs,
and whiffy fruit-bat drool!

Next it's the stinky-breath contest.
Max wins without a doubt.

He turns the air thick yellow-green,
and all his friends pass out.

In messy monster hide-and-seek,
Max hides inside a bin,

and as a great disguise, he wears
an old banana skin.

"Whoopee!" Max cries. "It's time for tea!
These termite tarts taste yummy.

"Mmm! Glow-worm wraps and earwig rolls,
and cockroach crisps — so scrummy!"

Out comes the eyeball birthday cake
(that SQUELCHES when you chew!).

Max blows his earwax candles out,
then gobbles them down too!

"Monster food fight!" someone shouts.
The monsters duck and dodge.

The maggot cream goes flying,
and hits them all — SPLAT! SPLODGE!

TA-DAH! It's DRAGON jelly time,
their scrumptious, sizzling treat.

It's red. It's wobbly. Best of all,
it's SCARY HOT to eat!

The bubbling jelly's gobbled down,
the monsters shake and hiss.

SWOOSH! Dragon jelly is so h-hot, smoke shoots out — just like this!

The monsters take home goody bags.
Yippee! Guess what they get?

A teeny, fiery DRAGON each —
the PERFECT monster pet!

For yuck-loving little monsters, everywhere! ~ CF

For Jake ~ SH

Bloomsbury Publishing, London, New Delhi, New York and Sydney
First published in Great Britain in 2014 by Bloomsbury Publishing Plc
50 Bedford Square, London, WC1B 3DP

Text copyright © Claire Freedman 2014
Illustrations copyright © Sue Hendra 2014
The moral rights of the author and illustrator have been asserted

A CIP catalogue record of this book is available from the British Library

ISBN 978 1 4088 3883 9 (HB)
ISBN 978 1 4088 3884 6 (PB)
ISBN 978 1 4088 4619 3 (eBook)

1 3 5 7 9 10 8 6 4 2

Printed in China by Leo Paper Products, Heshan, Guangdong

All papers used by Bloomsbury Publishing are natural, recyclable products made from
wood grown in well-managed forests. The manufacturing processes conform
to the environmental regulations of the country of origin

www.bloomsbury.com

BLOOMSBURY is a registered trademark of Bloomsbury Publishing Plc